VICENTE EL VALIENTE

★

BIG BRAVE BRIAN

★

M.P. Robertson

F
FRANCES LINCOLN
CHILDREN'S BOOKS

Vicente el Valiente

es el hombre más valiente del mundo.

Para mi papá, Ken el Valiente, que no le tiene miedo a nada,
con la excepción de mi mamá, la pequeña pero beligerante Olive.

For my dad, Big Brave Ken, who isn't afraid of anything,
apart from my mum, Little Belligerent Olive.

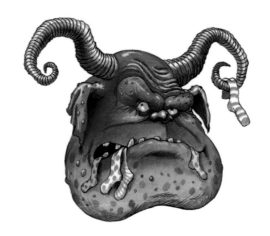

Big Brave Brian copyright © Frances Lincoln Limited 2007
English text and illustrations copyright © M.P. Robertson 2007

Spanish translation copyright © Frances Lincoln Limited 2007
Translation into Spanish by Esther Sarfatti

This edition published in Great Britain and in the USA in 2008 by
Frances Lincoln Children's Books, 4 Torriano Mews,
Torriano Avenue, London NW5 2RZ

www.franceslincoln.com

British Library Cataloguing in Publication Data available on request

ISBN 978-1-84507-857-7

The illustrations in this book are watercolour and black pen

Set in HooskerDont

Printed in Singapore

1 3 5 7 9 8 6 4 2

You can find out more about the books by M.P. Robertson
on his website: www.mprobertson.co.uk

Para mi papá, Ken el Valiente, que no le tiene miedo a nada,
con la excepción de mi mamá, la pequeña pero beligerante Olive.

For my dad, Big Brave Ken, who isn't afraid of anything,
apart from my mum, Little Belligerent Olive.

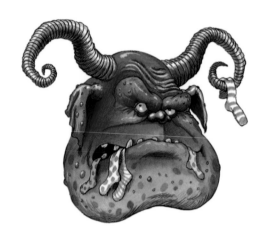

Big Brave Brian copyright © Frances Lincoln Limited 2007
English text and illustrations copyright © M.P. Robertson 2007

Spanish translation copyright © Frances Lincoln Limited 2007
Translation into Spanish by Esther Sarfatti

This edition published in Great Britain and in the USA in 2008 by
Frances Lincoln Children's Books, 4 Torriano Mews,
Torriano Avenue, London NW5 2RZ

www.franceslincoln.com

British Library Cataloguing in Publication Data available on request

ISBN 978-1-84507-857-7

The illustrations in this book are watercolour and black pen

Set in HooskerDont

Printed in Singapore

1 3 5 7 9 8 6 4 2

You can find out more about the books by M.P. Robertson
on his website: www.mprobertson.co.uk

Big Brave Brian is the bravest man in the world.

Los osos pardos gruñones

que viven debajo de los escalones
nada pueden contra Vicente el Valiente.

Grumpy Grizzly Bears

that live beneath the stairs
are no match for Big Brave Brian.

Vicente el Valiente no teme a los

horripilantes monstruos
del pantano

que son el terror del cuarto de baño.

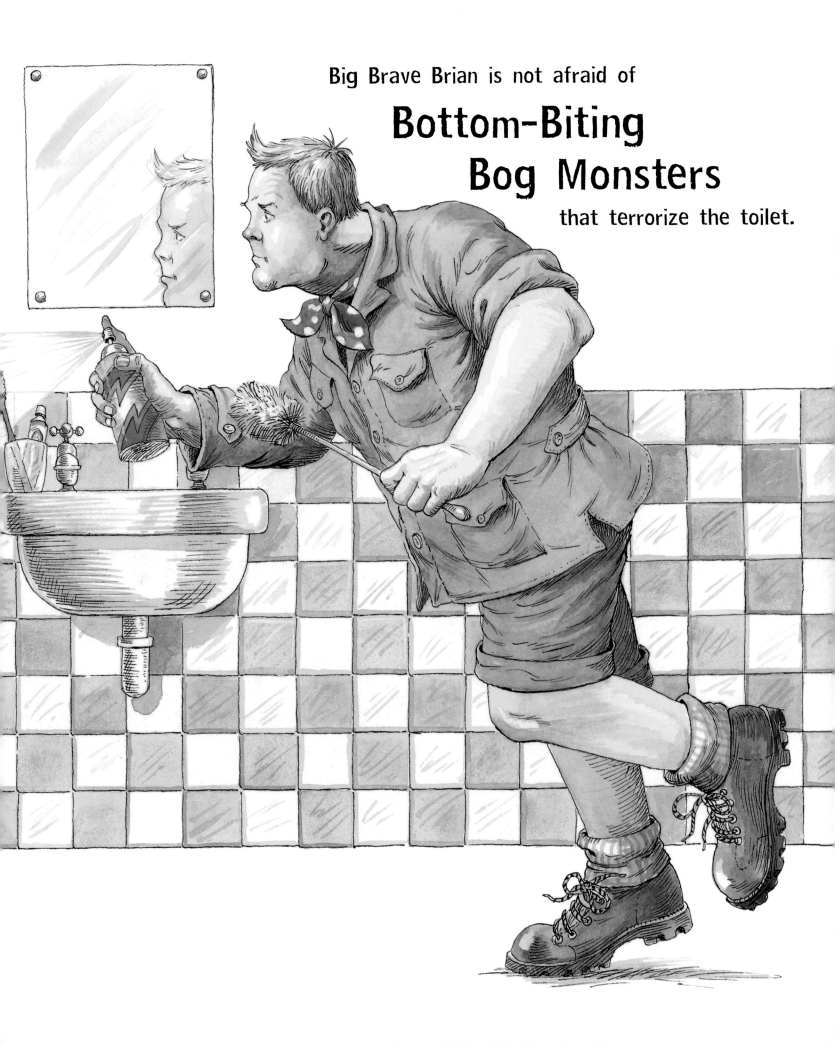

Big Brave Brian is not afraid of

Bottom-Biting Bog Monsters

that terrorize the toilet.

Las arañitas pequeñitas
Incy Wincy Spiders

que suben por las cañerías no asustan a Vicente el Valiente.

that climb up the spout don't frighten Big Brave Brian.

Las babosas gigantes y viscosas
que beben el agua de la bañera cual sopa
no preocupan a Vicente en absoluto.

Slime-Slurpin' Slug Creatures
that drink his bathwater like soup
hold no fear for Brian.

Los gigantes

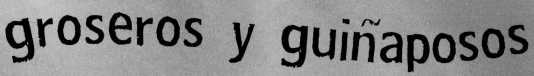

groseros y guiñaposos

que observan a Vicente por la ventana
no le ponen los pelos de punta.

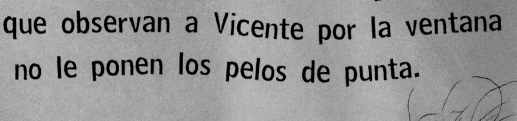

Ghastly Gawping Giants

that stare through
his bedroom window
don't make Brian's
knees knock.

Los trasgos traviesos

devoradores de ositos de peluche

no ponen nervioso a Vicente.

Teddy Gobbling Goblins that tumble from the toy chest don't give Brian the collywobbles.

Los seres que hacen extraños ruidos en la noche no hacen a Vicente perder la calma.

Things that go Bump in the Night don't give Brian the heebie-jeebies.

Los demonios devora-medias

que acechan debajo de la cama
no atemorizan a Vicente el Valiente.

Sock-Munching Demons

that lurk under the bed
don't scare Big Brave Brian.

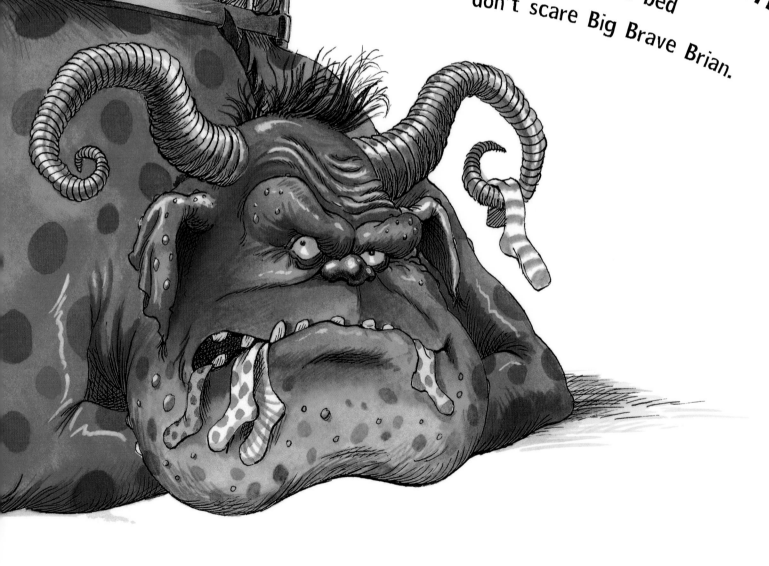

Pero existe una cosa que incluso a
Vicente el Valiente
le da miedo...

But there is one thing that even
Big Brave Brian
is scared of...